STAR WARS®

TREASURY

THE ORIGINAL TRILOGY

EGMONT
We bring stories to life

EGMONT
We bring stories to life

First published in Great Britain 2015 by Egmont UK Limited
The Yellow Building, 1 Nicholas Road, London W11 4AN

Written by Ryder Windham
Designed by Richard Hull and Maddox Philpot
Illustrated by Brian Rood

© & ™ 2015 Lucasfilm Ltd.
ISBN 978 1 4052 8022 8
62949/1
Printed in Italy

To find more great *Star Wars* books, visit www.egmont.co.uk/starwars

Stay safe online. Any website addresses listed in this book are correct at the time of going to print. However, Egmont is not responsible for content hosted by third parties. Please be aware that online content can be subject to change and websites can contain content that is unsuitable for children. We advise that all children are supervised when using the internet.

Egmont is passionate about helping to preserve the world's remaining ancient forests. We only use paper from legal and sustainable forest sources. This book is made from paper certified by the Forest Stewardship Council® (FSC®), an organisation dedicated to promoting responsible management of forest resources. For more information on the FSC, please visit www.fsc.org. To learn more about Egmont's sustainable paper policy, please visit www.egmont.co.uk/ethical

STAR WARS®

TREASURY
THE ORIGINAL TRILOGY

RYDER WINDHAM

BASED ON THE STORIES BY
GEORGE LUCAS

AND SCREENPLAYS BY
**GEORGE LUCAS, LAWRENCE KASDAN
AND LEIGH BRACKETT**

ILLUSTRATIONS BY
BRIAN ROOD

A LONG TIME AGO IN A GALAXY FAR, FAR AWAY .....

CONTENTS

STAR WARS®

EPISODE IV
A NEW HOPE

IT IS A PERIOD OF CIVIL WAR. Rebel spaceships, striking from a hidden base, have won their first victory against the evil Galactic Empire.

During the battle, rebel spies managed to steal secret plans to the Empire's ultimate weapon, the Death Star, an armoured space station with enough power to destroy an entire planet.

Pursued by the Empire's sinister agents, Princess Leia races home aboard her starship, custodian of the stolen plans that can save her people and restore freedom to the galaxy ...

BURSTS OF LASERFIRE
streaked after a lone starship, which was being chased by an immense Imperial Star Destroyer.

Both vessels had just entered Tatooine's orbit when the Star Destroyer scored a direct hit on the smaller ship's sensor array. Without a starboard shield or power to its engines, the *Tantive IV* was effectively crippled.

INSIDE THE BATTERED SHIP,

C-3PO, a gold-plated humanoid protocol droid, and his counterpart, R2-D2, an astromech, were very worried.

'Did you hear that?' C-3PO said. 'They've shut down the main reactor. We'll be destroyed for sure. This is madness!'

Suddenly, sparks blazed at the entry door! The hatch exploded. Before the smoke cleared, white-armoured Imperial stormtroopers charged through, firing their blasters at the rebels. The rebels fought back, and the corridor was filled with deadly, crisscrossing blaster fire.

A SQUAD OF STORMTROOPERS

secured the corridor, then moved away from the hatch as a tall, caped figure entered. He was clad entirely in black. He was Darth Vader, Lord of the Sith.

Vader surveyed the fallen rebels on the corridor floor. Stepping over the bodies, Darth Vader proceeded into the rebel ship.

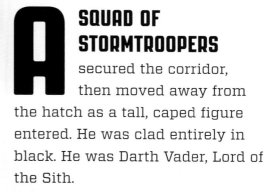

R2-D2 WAS WITH PRINCESS LEIA, who had called for him. She inserted a data card into a slot beneath R2-D2's radar eye.

From nearby, C-3PO cried, 'Artoo, where are you?'

While Leia crept off to hide, R2-D2 moved towards C-3PO's voice.

'At last!' C-3PO said when he saw R2-D2. 'Where have you been? They're heading in this direction. What are we going to do? We'll be sent to the spice mines of Kessel or smashed into who knows what!'

R2-D2 rolled away from C-3PO, heading for the escape pod access tunnel.

'Wait a minute,' C-3PO said. 'Where are you going?'

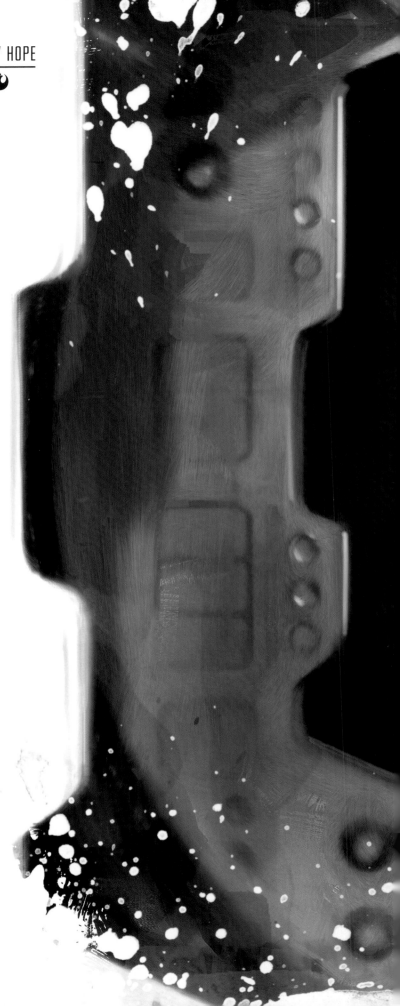

DARTH VADER and an Imperial officer confronted Princess Leia, who was now a prisoner.

'Darth Vader,' Leia said. 'Only you could be so bold.'

'Don't act so surprised, Your Highness,' Vader said. 'Several transmissions were beamed to this ship by rebel spies. I want to know what happened to the plans they sent you.'

'I don't know what you're talking about,' Leia said, feigning innocence. 'I'm a member of the Imperial Senate on a diplomatic mission to Alderaan …'

'You are a part of the Rebel Alliance … and a traitor,' Vader snarled. 'Take her away!'

As Vader walked away, Imperial Commander Praji stopped him and said, 'Lord Vader, an escape pod was jettisoned during the fighting, but no life-forms were aboard.'

Vader said, 'She must have hidden the plans in the escape pod. Send a detachment down to retrieve them. See to it personally, Commander. There'll be no one to stop us this time.'

C-3PO AND R2-D2 were trudging down a steep dune, leaving behind their life-pod. C-3PO sighed. R2-D2 whistled and made a sharp right turn.

'Where do you think you're going?' C-3PO asked.

R2-D2 answered with a stream of electronic noise.

'Well, I'm not going that way,' C-3PO said. 'It's much too rocky. This way is much easier.'

The astromech uttered more beeps and whistles.

'What mission?' C-3PO said, dumbfounded. 'What are you talking about? I've just about had enough of you! Go that way! You'll be malfunctioning within a day, you nearsighted scrap pile!'

When he realised C-3PO was determined to go his own way, R2-D2 turned his dome in the other direction and moved off towards the rocks.

R2-D2 KEPT MOVING. He was on a mission, so he rolled forward on his treads, proceeding cautiously through a rock canyon.

A pair of lights flickered between two boulders, then winked off. R2-D2 paused. Suddenly, a squat, hooded figure with glowing eyes jumped out from the shadows and fired a blaster at R2-D2! The astromech shrieked as rippling charges of electricity travelled over and through his body. He pitched forward and crashed against the hard ground.

The Jawa called out to the surrounding shadows, and seven more Jawas scurried from their hiding places. The Jawas picked up R2-D2 and carried the droid to their waiting transport.

A **SQUAD** of Imperial stormtroopers found the abandoned escape pod half buried in the sand.

'Someone was in the pod,' the lead trooper said. He raised a pair of macrobinoculars to his helmet's lenses and scanned the desert, then added, 'The tracks go off in this direction.'

Another stormtrooper bent down to lift a shiny metal disk from the sand. Holding it up for inspection, the stormtrooper said, 'Look, sir – droids.'

THE JAWA TRANSPORT, called a sandcrawler, was an enormous rust-covered vehicle. Inside, R2 found his friend, C-3PO, who had also been abducted by the Jawas. The Jawas herded C-3PO, R2-D2 and several other droids down the sandcrawler's main ramp. They had arrived at the spot where Luke Skywalker lived on a moisture farm.

He and his Uncle Owen had decided to purchase two droids. The first they chose was C-3PO. The second, a red one, started to come with them – and then exploded!

Turning to the Jawa, Owen said, 'What about that blue one? We'll take that one.'

C-3PO said, 'I'm quite sure you'll be very pleased with that one, sir. He really is in first-class condition. I've worked with him before.'

THE DROIDS FOLLOWED LUKE

into the moisture farm – their new home. Luke knelt beside R2-D2 and began cleaning him.

'Hello,' Luke said to R2-D2.

R2-D2 beeped.

Luke was scraping R2-D2's head carefully with a pick when a fragment broke loose with a snap, and Luke looked up to see a flickering three-dimensional hologram of a young woman being projected from R2-D2's dome. The hologram said, 'Help me, Obi-Wan Kenobi. You're my only hope.'

'Who is she?' Luke said in awe. 'She's beautiful.'

C-3PO said, 'I'm afraid I'm not quite sure, sir. Artoo says that he's the property of Obi-Wan Kenobi, a resident of these parts. And it's a private message for him.'

LUKE LEFT THE GARAGE and crossed the courtyard floor to the dining alcove. He sat down at the table and said, 'You know, I think that R2 unit we bought might have been stolen.'

Owen glowered. 'What makes you think that?'

'Well, I stumbled across a recording while I was cleaning him,' Luke said. 'He says he belongs to someone called Obi-Wan Kenobi.'

Hearing this name, Owen and Luke's aunt, Beru, exchanged nervous glances. Chewing his food thoughtfully, Luke added, 'I thought he might have meant old Ben.'

'That wizard's just a crazy old man,' Owen said.

LUKE STEPPED OUT of the homestead's entrance dome and kicked at the sand. He couldn't stop thinking about Biggs Darklighter, his best friend. He'd seen Biggs just the day before, at the Anchorhead power station. Biggs had returned to Tatooine to tell Luke he'd graduated from the Academy. He'd also confided that he intended to jump ship and join the Rebel Alliance.

Luke stopped to watch Tatooine's giant twin suns set over a distant dune range. The hot wind tugged at his tunic. He felt trapped and longed for adventure.

THE NEXT MORNING Luke's sand-blasted landspeeder raced over the desert. R2-D2 had run away the night before and Luke had to find him – quickly! Luke checked the autoscan on the dashboard's scopes. 'Look,' he said to C-3PO. 'There's a droid on the scanner. Dead ahead. Might be our little R2 unit. Hit the accelerator.'

LUKE AND C-3PO found R2-D2 trudging along the floor of a massive canyon. Suddenly, R2-D2 emitted a flurry of frantic whistles and screams.

C-3PO translated: 'There are several creatures approaching from the southeast.'

'Sand People!' Luke gasped. 'Or worse!'

Luke climbed a ridge to get a better look but was ambushed by a hidden Sand Person. Three Sand People hauled Luke's unconscious body down to the canyon floor and dumped him beside some rocks; then they began to strip the vehicle, tossing parts and supplies in all directions.

But when a great howling moan echoed through the canyon, the three Sand People fled from the scene. An old man appeared. Luke stirred and his eyes widened. 'Ben? Ben Kenobi?'

THE OLD MAN was indeed Obi-Wan (Ben) Kenobi. His house was a dome-roofed hovel. Inside, Obi-Wan explained to Luke, 'I was once a Jedi Knight, the same as your father.' He removed a shiny object from a trunk. 'Your father wanted you to have this when you were old enough, but your uncle wouldn't allow it.'

Luke asked, 'What is it?'

'Your father's lightsaber,' Ben said. 'This is the weapon of a Jedi Knight.'

Luke asked, 'How did my father die?'

Obi-Wan said, 'A young Jedi named Darth Vader helped the Empire hunt down and destroy the Jedi Knights. He betrayed and murdered your father.'

As Ben touched R2-D2's dome, his hologram projector flicked on.

'General Kenobi,' said Princess Leia's hologram, 'years ago you served my father in the Clone Wars. Now he begs you to help him in his struggle against the Empire. I have placed information vital to the survival of the Rebellion into the memory systems of this Artoo unit. You must see this droid safely delivered to him on Alderaan. Help me, Obi-Wan Kenobi. You're my only hope.'

Ben looked at Luke and said, 'You must learn the ways of the Force if you're to come with me to Alderaan.'

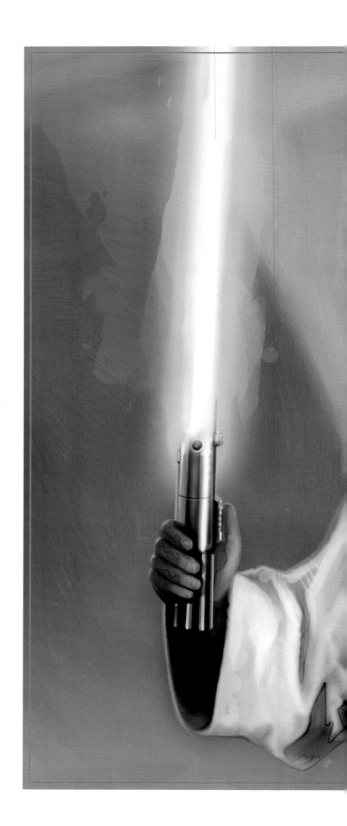

DARTH VADER travelled by Star Destroyer to deliver Princess Leia Organa to the Death Star.

'Until this battle station is fully operational, we are vulnerable,' said Commander Tagge. 'The Rebel Alliance is more dangerous than you realise.'

Admiral Motti sneered, 'Dangerous to your starfleet, Commander – not to this battle station!'

'If the rebels have obtained a complete technical readout of this station,' countered Tagge, 'it is possible, however unlikely, that they might find a weakness and exploit it.'

From beside Grand Moff Tarkin, Darth Vader said, 'The plans you refer to will soon be back in our hands.'

When Motti mocked Vader and the Force, the Sith Lord used the Force to choke him until Tarkin ordered Vader to release him.

'This bickering is pointless,' Tarkin said. 'Lord Vader will provide us with the location of the rebel fortress by the time this station is operational. We will then crush the Rebellion with one swift stroke.'

LUKE, BEN AND THE TWO DROIDS were speeding across Tatooine when they came upon what was left of the Jawa sandcrawler. Dozens of Jawas lay dead, their small forms scattered across the sand.

Luke said, 'These are the same Jawas that sold us the droids.'

Ben pointed out that only Imperial stormtroopers were so precise in their attacks. An awful realisation hit Luke: 'If they traced the robots here, they may have learned who they sold them to, and that would lead them back … home!'

Luke jumped into the landspeeder and sped away from the burning sandcrawler. He saw the rising smoke from kilometres away. The Lars homestead was consumed by a fiery blaze. His aunt and uncle were dead. There was nothing left for Luke on Tatooine. He told Ben that he would go with him to Alderaan.

ON THE DEATH

Star, Darth Vader interrogated Princess Leia. 'And now, Your Highness, we will discuss the location of your hidden rebel base.'

There was an electronic hum from behind Vader; then a spherical black droid hovered slowly into the cell. It was an interrogator droid. Leia's eyes widened with fear. The droid extended its syringe and hovered towards her.

The cell door slammed and the interrogation began.

APPROACHING MOS EISLEY spaceport, Luke slowed the landspeeder. Suddenly, five white-armoured stormtroopers noticed C-3PO and R2-D2.

The squad leader said, 'Let me see your identification.'

'You don't need to see his identification,' Ben said, using the Force.

Looking at his fellow stormtroopers, the squad leader said, 'We don't need to see his identification.'

Ben said, 'These aren't the droids you're looking for.'

'These aren't the droids we're looking for,' the squad leader repeated, and waved them through.

Luke drove the landspeeder away from the stormtroopers.

'I'M READY FOR ANYTHING,' Luke said as he followed Ben into the cantina. They were looking for a ship to take them to Alderaan.

The bartender was scowling at Luke when an alien spat out, 'Negola dewaghi wooldugger!'

A disfigured man said, 'He doesn't like you.'

Ben said calmly, 'This little one's not worth the effort. Come, let me get you something.'

The man with the disfigured face suddenly flung Luke away from the bar. Luke crashed into a nearby table, and his attackers reached for their blaster pistols.

Ben drew his lightsaber. The blade flashed on and swept past the blaster-wielding criminals. The disfigured man had a deep slash across his chest. The alien screamed and his right arm fell to the floor, still clutching its blaster.

The entire fight had lasted only seconds.

BEN NODDED at a gigantic furry Wookiee and said to Luke, 'Chewbacca here is first mate on a ship that might suit us.'

Chewbacca sat down with them in a private booth. They were soon joined by Han Solo, who said, 'I'm captain of the *Millennium Falcon*. Chewie here tells me you're looking for passage to the Alderaan system.'

'Yes, indeed,' Ben said. 'If it's a fast ship.'

'Fast ship?' Han said. 'You've never heard of the *Millennium Falcon*? I've outrun Imperial starships. She's fast enough for you, old man.'

After payment was agreed upon, Han said, 'Okay. You guys got yourselves a ship. Docking Bay Ninety-four.'

INSIDE DOCKING BAY 94

were a number of gangsters and at least one bounty hunter.

'Solo,' Jabba the Hutt bellowed at the *Falcon*. 'Come out of there, Solo!'

'Right here, Jabba,' Han called from behind the Hutt. 'I've been waiting for you.'

Jabba wanted Han to pay back money for a smuggling job that had failed.

'Look, Jabba. Even I get boarded sometimes,' Solo said. 'You think I had a choice? I'll pay you back plus a little extra. I just need a little more time.'

Jabba said, 'Han, my boy, you're the best. But if you fail me again, I'll put a price on your head so big you won't be able to go near a civilised system.'

Chewbacca followed Han into the *Falcon*.

PRINCESS LEIA was brought to the control room of the Death Star.

'Governor Tarkin,' Leia said. 'I recognised your foul stench when I was brought on board.'

Tarkin smiled. 'Charming to the last. Princess Leia, before your execution I would like you to be my guest at a ceremony that will make this battle station operational. No star system will dare oppose the Emperor now.'

She said, 'The more you tighten your grip, Tarkin, the more star systems will slip through your fingers.'

'Not after we demonstrate the power of this station,' Tarkin informed her with confidence. 'Since you are reluctant to provide us with the location of the rebel base, I have chosen to test this station's destructive power ... on your home planet of Alderaan.'

Leia begged Tarkin to spare her peaceful planet, but he did not listen. In one explosive instant, Alderaan was gone.

IN THE *MILLENNIUM FALCON'S* hold, Luke was testing his lightsaber skills against a remote. His eyes followed the remote, but his movements were stiff.

Ben placed a helmet over Luke's head and lowered the blast shield so it covered his eyes. 'This time, let go of your conscious self and act on instinct.'

Luke laughed. 'I can't even see. How am I supposed to fight?'

'Your eyes can deceive you,' Ben said. 'Don't trust them.'

Luke relaxed and … somehow, he sensed the remote's movements. The remote fired three bursts and Luke blocked each shot.

'That's good,' Ben told him. 'You have taken your first step into a larger world.'

THE *FALCON* dropped out of hyperspace into realspace.

Han said, 'Our position is correct, except ... no Alderaan! It ain't there. It's been totally blown away.'

'What? How?' Luke asked.

'Destroyed ... by the Empire!' Ben said.

An alarm sounded and Han glanced at a sensor scope. An Imperial TIE fighter streaked past the *Falcon*.

'If they identify us, we're in big trouble,' Luke said.

Han said, 'Chewie – jam its transmissions.'

'Look at him,' Luke said. 'He's heading for that small moon.'

'That's no moon! It's a space station,' Ben said.

The *Falcon* began to shake violently. 'We're caught in a tractor beam!' Han explained. 'It's pulling us in.'

TARKIN AND DARTH VADER were in the Death Star conference room when an intercom buzzed. An officer announced, 'We've captured a freighter. Its markings match those of a ship that blasted its way out of Mos Eisley.'

Vader said, 'They must be trying to return the stolen plans to the princess. She may yet be of some use to us.'

As Vader entered the hangar, an officer said, 'There's no one on board, sir. According to the log, the crew abandoned ship right after takeoff.'

'Send a scanning crew aboard,' Vader ordered. 'I want every part of the ship checked.'

Then Vader said to himself, 'I sense something … a presence I've not felt since …'

Then it hit him.

Obi-Wan Kenobi.

NSIDE THE *FALCON*, Luke, Han and the others emerged from their hiding place. Then the group split up. Obi-Wan went to turn off the tractor beam so they could leave. The droids stayed near the hangar, while Han, Luke and Chewie decided to rescue the princess.

In stormtrooper disguises, Luke and Han escorted Chewbacca through a Death Star corridor. The lift door opened and they stepped in. Han pressed the button for level five and said, 'This is not going to work.'

'Why didn't you say so before?' Luke said.

'I *did* say so before!' Han protested.

ON THE DETENTION LEVEL, Chewbacca roared and lashed out, smashing a guard. Then Han and Luke blasted the other Imperial troops. Han scanned a data screen. 'Here it is … twenty-one eighty-seven. You go and get the princess. I'll hold them here.'

Luke ran up the steps and entered the corridor. He slapped a button on the wall and the cell door slid up. Princess Leia was sleeping. She opened her eyes and said, 'Aren't you a little short for a stormtrooper?'

'Huh?' Luke replied. 'Oh … the uniform.' He pulled off his helmet. 'I'm Luke Skywalker. I'm here to rescue you. I've got your R2 unit. I'm here with Ben Kenobi.'

'Ben Kenobi!' Leia cried, jumping up. 'Where is he?'

Luke said, 'Come on!'

TO **ESCAPE** the other stormtroopers, Han, Leia, Luke and Chewie jumped into a garbage chute. They landed in a deep pile of trash.

'It could be worse,' Leia said.

The walls rumbled and suddenly pushed inward. It was worse.

Leia said to Han, 'Try and brace it with something!'

'Wait a minute!' Luke cried, and reached for his comlink transmitter. 'See-Threepio. Come in, See-Threepio!'

C-3PO said into the transmitter, 'We've had some problems –'

Luke interrupted. 'Shut down all the garbage mashers on the detention level!'

At the last moment, the walls stopped. R2-D2 had plugged into the main computer and told it to stop them. The little droid had saved the day!

AFTER GETTING OUT of the trash compactor, Han and Luke removed their stormtrooper armour. They walked down a hallway; then, as the group rounded a corner, they ran straight into several approaching stormtroopers.

'It's them!' shouted the squad leader. 'Blast them!'

Han fired and charged the startled troopers, who turned and ran back up the hallway. As Han chased and fired at the troopers, he shouted to his friends, 'Get back to the ship!'

LUKE AND LEIA were spotted by yet another squad of stormtroopers. They raced up a ramp and were through a doorway before they realised the floor ended at an enormous air shaft.

'I think we took a wrong turn,' Luke said.

Across the chasm, another open doorway beckoned them. Blaster fire exploded behind them. Leia hit a switch and the door slid shut. While she fended off more troopers, who were shooting at them from above, Luke pulled a grappling hook from his belt. He tossed the hook high and it whipped around a pipe.

Leia kissed Luke's cheek and said, 'For luck!'

They swung across the abyss and landed on the opposite ledge.

HAN AND CHEWBACCA raced through a corridor with many stormtroopers hot on their trail. They ran into the hangar and saw the *Falcon* with its landing ramp still down.

'Didn't we just leave this party?' Han said. He then saw Leia and Luke rushing up from the other end of the hallway. 'What kept you?' he said.

'We ran into some old friends,' Leia joked, catching her breath.

Luke asked, 'Is the ship all right?'

'Seems okay, if we can get to it,' Han answered. 'Just hope the old man got the tractor beam out of commission.'

Inside the hangar, C-3PO turned to R2-D2 and said, 'Come on, Artoo, we're going!'

Then everyone ran for the *Falcon*'s landing ramp.

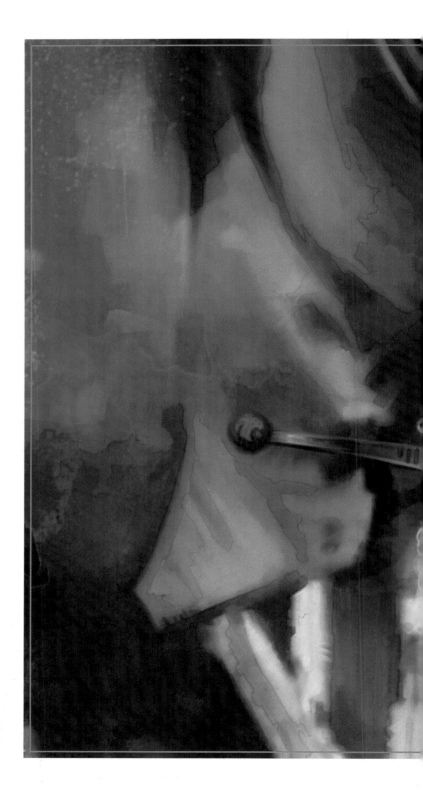

AT THE END of a tunnel leading to the hangar, Ben saw a tall, shadowy form. It was his former apprentice, Darth Vader.

'I've been waiting for you, Obi-Wan,' Vader said. 'The circle is now complete. When I left you, I was but the learner; now I am the master.'

'Only a master of evil, Darth,' Obi-Wan said.

There was a loud electric crackle as their lightsabers made contact.

'You can't win, Darth,' Obi-Wan said. 'If you strike me down, I shall become more powerful than you can possibly imagine.'

'Ben?' Luke asked as he came to a stop by the *Falcon*.

Ben looked at Luke and smiled; then he raised his lightsaber before him and closed his eyes. Vader's lightsaber swept through the air. Ben's cloak and lightsaber fell to the floor – but his body was gone.

From nowhere, Luke heard Ben's voice: 'Run, Luke! Run!'

WITH LUKE AND THE OTHERS

on board, the *Falcon* blasted away from the Death Star. In the main hold, Leia sat by Luke. He shook his head sadly and said, 'I can't believe he's gone.'

Han rushed into the hold. Looking at Luke, he said, 'Come on, buddy, we're not out of this yet!'

Luke followed Han to the gunport turrets. The *Falcon* shuddered as its shields took a laser hit from one of the four TIE fighters.

Han tracked one fighter and fired with his laser cannon, but missed. He got another TIE fighter in his sights and blasted laserbolts at it. The TIE fighter exploded. Luke swung the cannon and scored a direct hit. Another TIE fighter zoomed towards the *Falcon*, but Luke fired back and took that one out too. The last TIE fighter zoomed in. Han swivelled behind his laser cannon, and the ship was consumed in a fiery explosion.

Luke laughed. 'That's it! We did it!'

THE DEATH STAR followed the *Falcon* to Yavin 4. It was preparing to blow up the rebel base as soon as it was within range. Meanwhile, all the rebels had gathered to see if there was a way they could blow up the Death Star first.

'Its defences are designed around a direct large-scale assault,' General Dodonna said. 'A small one-man fighter should be able to penetrate the outer defence. An analysis of the plans provided by Princess Leia has demonstrated a weakness in the battle station.'

R2-D2 beeped proudly.

'The target area is only two meters wide,' Dodonna continued. 'It's a small thermal exhaust port. A precise hit will start a chain reaction which should destroy the station.'

A few minutes later, Luke climbed up the ladder to his X-wing.

HAN SOLO had to leave to pay Jabba the money he owed him. The X-wing and Y-wing starfighters sped away across space. Luke was flying low over the Death Star's surface when he heard Ben's voice again: 'Luke, trust your feelings.'

The battle was hard-fought. Soon, only Luke and a few other rebel pilots were still alive. He said to the others, 'We're going in full throttle. That ought to keep those fighters off our back.'

They followed Luke into the Death Star trench, where Imperial cannons opened fire.

Then Vader and the TIE fighters arrived.

'I'M ON THE LEADER,' Darth Vader told his wingmen.

The three TIE fighters sped after the lone X-wing that remained.

Luke adjusted the lens on his targeting scope. Just then, he heard Ben's voice: 'Use the Force, Luke.'

Darth Vader sensed the change. He said, 'The Force is strong in this one!'

Suddenly, an unexpected blast of laserfire struck one of the TIE fighters. It exploded. Vader exclaimed, 'What?' He glanced up.

It was the *Millennium Falcon*.

'Yahoo!' Han Solo hollered as he descended rapidly.

The *Falcon* raced towards the TIE fighters. Vader's wingman panicked and collided into Vader's TIE fighter before crashing into the side wall of the trench.

Vader fought to regain control of his fighter, but it continued to tumble across space.

LUKE LOOKED UP AND SMILED, then concentrated on the exhaust port. He looked at his targeting scope.

Ben's voice said, 'Luke, trust me.'

Luke reached towards his control panel and pressed a button. The targeting scope retracted and moved away from his helmet. Luke's action was detected by the controllers at the rebel base. A controller announced, 'His computer's off.' Addressing Luke directly, he said, 'You switched off your targeting computer. What's wrong?'

'Nothing,' Luke answered as he stayed on course for his target. 'I'm all right.'

He fired.

THE THREE SURVIVING REBEL STARFIGHTERS and the *Falcon* were barely out of the danger zone when the Death Star exploded in an immense, blinding flash.

'Great shot, kid,' Han said into his comm. 'That was one in a million.'

Luke let out a deep breath and relaxed. Ben's voice said, 'Remember, the Force will be with you … always.'

Luke smiled all the way back to Yavin 4.

N THE EXPANSIVE RUINS of the temple's throne room, hundreds of uniformed rebel troops stood at attention. Luke, Han and Chewbacca entered. When the trio arrived at the steps of the dais, the troops turned simultaneously on their heels to face the rebel leaders. Han bowed as Leia placed a medallion around his neck.

Luke glanced at C-3PO, who stood beside the rebel leaders. A happy beeping sound came from R2-D2. Leia placed a medallion around Luke's neck, too.

The ancient temple was suddenly filled with loud cheers and applause.

The battle against the Empire was far from over, but a small band of heroes had destroyed the Death Star – and won a great victory for the rebels!

83

IT IS A DARK TIME FOR THE REBELLION. Although

the Death Star has been destroyed, Imperial troops have driven the rebel forces from their hidden base and pursued them across the galaxy.

Evading the dreaded Imperial Starfleet, a group of freedom fighters led by Luke Skywalker has established a new secret base on the remote ice world of Hoth.

The evil lord Darth Vader, obsessed with finding young Skywalker, has dispatched thousands of remote probes into the far reaches of space …

SPEEDING THROUGH SPACE, a pod arrived in orbit of the ice world. The pod streaked downward until its journey ended on the planet's surface, smashing through layers of ice and snow.

As smoke billowed from the impact site and darkened the surrounding snow, the pod opened to reveal the probot's armoured form. Activating its repulsorlift, the black probot rose through the smoke and immediately went to work. Its sensors scanned for Rebel Alliance transmissions and signs of life and habitation. It then moved on, gliding noiselessly through the chilled air … unknowingly getting closer and closer to the rebel base.

LUKE SKYWALKER RODE his two-legged snow lizard, a tauntaun, over a windswept ice slope on Hoth.

'Echo Three to Echo Seven,' Luke said into the comlink. 'Han, old buddy, do you read me? I don't pick up any life readings.'

'There isn't enough life on this ice cube to fill a space cruiser,' Han Solo commented over the comlink. 'I'm going back.'

Luke switched off his comlink, and his tauntaun snorted nervously. 'Hey, steady, girl,' he said, reining back. 'Hey, what's the matter? You smell something?'

Suddenly, there was a monstrous howl. Luke turned quickly to face a massive wampa, its jaws flung open to display fiercely sharp teeth. A massive clawed hand slammed into Luke, knocking him from his saddle. He was unconscious before he hit the snow.

ECHO BASE, the secret location of the rebels on Hoth, was a vast network of passages and caves concealed within a glacial mountain. The base had quickly become home to several thousand rebel soldiers, technicians, droids and pilots.

The golden droid C-3PO and his astromech counterpart, R2-D2, were worried about Luke, who had not returned to the base.

'Princess Leia doesn't know where he is,' C-3PO said to Han. 'He hasn't come back yet.'

Han jumped onto a tauntaun's back and raced out of the cave into the dark night to search for Luke. The two droids stood with Leia near the base's entrance. With a loud boom, the giant heavy doors locked in place, sealing off the cavern from the freezing night. Chewbacca threw his head back and let out a suffering howl. Would they ever see Luke and Han again?

LUKE WAS HANGING upside down in a cave. His entire body hurt and he was very, very cold. He reached to his belt, but his lightsaber was gone. Luke spotted it beneath him, half buried in the snow. He stretched out his arm, but the lightsaber was beyond his reach.

Luke would have to use the Force! He extended his right hand towards the lightsaber. He tried to envision the weapon rising from the snow, but nothing happened.

Luke still didn't fully understand how to use the Force, but he had a feeling that he might be trying too hard. He closed his eyes and relaxed …

THE WAMPA LOOKED UP from its meal, sensing that something was wrong. In the other part of the cave, Luke again extended his hand. *The Force binds us …*

He heard the approaching wampa's heavy footsteps.

The lightsaber shot out of the snow and into Luke's hand. Its blue energy beam blazed to life. The wampa lunged for him as Luke freed himself and fell to the ground. Luke sprang to his feet just as the wampa was about to pounce, and wounded the monster with his lightsaber. He then ran out of the cave, pushing his way through snow and ice, tumbling smack into … a blizzard.

LUKE LAY FACEDOWN, nearly unconscious in the freezing snow. Suddenly, he heard a voice.

'Luke … Luke.'

Luke recognised the voice; could it be the Jedi Master who had been struck down by Darth Vader? Luke said aloud, 'Ben?' He lifted his head and could just make out the glowing form of his friend.

'You will go to the Dagobah system,' Ben Kenobi said. 'There you will learn from Yoda, the Jedi Master who instructed me.'

Obi-Wan Kenobi disappeared – but a lone tauntaun rider materialised where he had been, and approached Luke. It was Han Solo coming to the rescue!

LUKE WOKE UP in a transparent tank filled with warm liquid. He realised that he was in the Echo Base medical centre, and that the liquid in the tank was bacta, which healed wounds quickly. Then he saw his friends. Leia, Han, Chewbacca, R2-D2 and C-3PO were gathered on the other side of the medical centre's window. They waved to him. Still groggy, Luke returned the gesture, then felt his body being lifted out of the tank.

It was time to get back into action.

THE PROBOT WAS HEADING DOWN a ridge towards the rebel base when its sensors detected movement by a nearby snowbank – where a Wookiee's snow-covered head had just popped up.

Chewbacca ducked as the droid fired three rapid laser bursts. The laserbolts missed the Wookiee.

While the droid was distracted, Han rose from the other side and snapped off a quick shot. The droid responded by rotating its cylindrical body in midair and firing back at Han, but it missed. Han came up fast and fired a second blast at the droid, again hitting it. The droid exploded into smoke and flames.

Han said, 'It's a good bet the Empire knows we're here.'

DARTH VADER SAT inside his meditation chamber aboard his ship, the *Executor*. General Veers entered the chamber to deliver his latest report.

'My lord, the fleet has moved out of lightspeed,' Veers said. 'Comscan has detected an energy field protecting an area of the sixth planet of the Hoth system. The field is strong enough to deflect any bombardment.'

Vader seethed. 'The rebels are alerted to our presence. Admiral Ozzel came out of lightspeed too close to the system.'

Vader's seat rotated, allowing him to face a wide viewscreen. It flicked on and displayed an image of Admiral Ozzel on the bridge. Using the Force, Vader strangled him.

'You have failed me for the last time, Admiral,' Vader said as Ozzel fell to the ground.

OUTSIDE THE HANGAR

at Echo Base on Hoth, hundreds of rebel troops took up their positions in a series of long snow trenches. Dots suddenly appeared on the horizon. An officer looked through a pair of electrobinoculars and saw that the dots were in fact colossal Imperial walkers!

The rhythmic pounding of the walkers' lumbering footsteps made the ground vibrate beneath the rebels' feet.

Meanwhile, rebel pilots in the hangar ran to their snowspeeders, but the five walkers kept coming, blasting everything that got in their way. Would the rebels ever be able to stop them?

THE REBEL SNOWSPEEDERS

flew low over the trenches, where troops were firing at the approaching walkers. Luke's call sign was Rogue Leader, and he headed up Rogue Squadron. 'All right, boys, keep tight now,' Luke said to the other Rogues.

The walkers' heads were attached to flexible armoured necks, and the heads moved easily to fire at the incoming snowspeeders. Red energy bolts whizzed past the evasive speeders, which began wrapping the walkers' legs with cables in hopes of tripping the giant machines. One enormous walker tried to step forward, but the cable had so tangled its legs that it began to topple. It crashed heavily onto the icy ground.

In the trenches, the troops cheered at the sight of the fallen walker. A trench officer shouted, 'Come on!'

BUT THE BATTLE RAGED ON. The Imperial walkers fired lasers as they lumbered onward and continued their slow, steady assault on the rebel base. Another rebel gun tower was destroyed, then another and another.

Inside his own walker, General Veers studied various readouts on his control console. His walker was almost within firing range of the rebels' generator. He said, 'Prepare to target the main generator.'

Back in the trenches, the situation had become dire.

'Begin retreat!' shouted the rebel trench officer.

IN HIS WALKER, General Veers spoke to a hologram of Darth Vader: 'I've reached the main power generators. The shield will be down in moments. You may start your landing.'

The walker fired energy beams from its laser cannons and blew the generator sky-high.

Inside the rebel base, C-3PO was running after Leia and Han. 'Wait! Wait!' the droid cried as he followed them up the landing ramp of the *Millennium Falcon*.

'Punch it!' Han ordered in the cockpit, and Chewie hit the accelerator. The ship launched forward.

Darth Vader arrived in the hangar just in time to see the *Falcon* soar out the mouth of the cave and vanish into the sky.

THE *MILLENNIUM FALCON* wasn't able to leave Hoth easily. The moment the ship entered space, it had four TIE fighters and one enormous Star Destroyer on its tail. Green laser fire streaked from the TIE fighters, hammering the *Falcon*'s shields.

Inside the *Falcon*'s cockpit, Chewbacca checked the deflector shields, which were taking a pounding. The Wookiee let out a loud howl.

Han answered, 'I saw 'em! I saw 'em!'

'Saw what?' Leia said from the seat behind him.

'Star Destroyers,' Han explained. 'Two of them, coming right at us.'

WITH ONE STAR DESTROYER directly behind it, the *Falcon* headed straight for the two oncoming cruisers. When the *Falcon* was between the two vessels, Han Solo threw his ship into a steep dive, then guided the *Falcon* through a dizzying spiral to evade the laser-firing TIE fighters.

'Prepare to make the jump to lightspeed!' Han shouted to Chewbacca.

But nothing happened. Han examined the controls and muttered, 'I think we're in trouble.'

'If I may say so, sir,' C-3PO said, 'I noticed earlier the hyperdrive motivator has been damaged. It's impossible to go to lightspeed!'

'We're in trouble!' Han said.

SUDDENLY THE *FALCON* was hit by something that wasn't laser fire. Solo glanced at the sensor monitors. Asteroids!

Without hesitation, Han said, 'Chewie, set two-seven-one.'

'What are you doing?' Leia said to Han. 'You're not actually going into an asteroid field!'

'They'd be crazy to follow us, wouldn't they?' Han pointed out, guiding his ship past more asteroids.

A large asteroid whizzed past the cockpit. One TIE fighter swooped straight into an asteroid and exploded.

Out the cockpit window, Han saw a gaping crater on the surface of an especially large asteroid. He circled back, then swung the *Falcon* into a dive that deposited them into the crater … and total darkness.

LUKE SKYWALKER had escaped Hoth in his X-wing starfighter. Now he was in space, gazing at a strange, cloud-covered world. He said to R2-D2, 'Yes, that's it. Dagobah.'

As they began their descent towards Dagobah, an alarm began to buzz,, and R2-D2 beeped frantically.

'I know, I know!' Luke said. 'I can't see a thing! Just hang on.'

There was a series of thrashing and cracking sounds, and Luke realised his ship was crashing through the upper branches of tall trees. Then, with a sudden jolt, the X-wing came to a stop. Luke had landed in a watery swamp. He climbed out of his cockpit and onto the shore. Now he had to find Yoda.

● ● ● ● ● ● ● ●

LUKE SCRAMBLED OVER slippery moss and plants. He sighed as he looked around. 'This place gives me the creeps. I feel like –'

'Feel like what?' a croaking voice interrupted.

Luke's blaster flashed from its holster.

'Away put your weapon!' the creature said as he threw his arms up over his face. 'I mean you no harm.' He wore a ratty old robe. The creature asked, 'I am wondering, why are you here?'

'I'm looking for someone,' Luke answered warily. 'I'm looking for a Jedi Master.'

The creature's eyes widened. 'Oohhh, Jedi Master. Yoda. You seek Yoda. Mmm. Take you to him, I will.' The creature laughed.

R2-D2 watched Luke follow the weird creature into a mysterious land.

THE *MILLENNIUM FALCON* had touched down inside the asteroid cave. Han said, 'I'm going to shut down everything but the emergency power systems.'

Leia was trying to repair a part of the *Falcon* when Han interrupted her. Leia was angry with him. 'You make it so difficult sometimes.'

'I do, I really do,' Han agreed. 'You could be a little nicer, though. Come on, admit it. Sometimes you think I'm all right.'

'Occasionally,' Leia admitted. 'Maybe. When you aren't acting like a scoundrel.'

'You like me because I'm a scoundrel,' Han said. 'There aren't enough scoundrels in your life.'

'I happen to like nice men,' Leia told him.

Han replied softly, 'I'm a nice man.'

'No, you're not. You're –'

He kissed her.

119

A BOARD THE *EXECUTOR,* Darth Vader kneeled before a hologram of the Emperor. The Emperor said, 'We have a new enemy – the young rebel who destroyed the Death Star. I have no doubt this boy is the offspring of Anakin Skywalker.'

'How is that possible?' Vader said.

'Search your feelings, Lord Vader. You will know it to be true. He could destroy us.'

'He's just a boy,' Vader said. 'Obi-Wan can no longer help him.'

'The Force is strong with him,' the Emperor said. 'The son of Skywalker must not become a Jedi.'

Vader said, 'If he could be turned, he would become a powerful ally.'

'Yes,' said the Emperor. 'Can it be done?'

'He will join us or die, Master,' Vader said. He bowed, and the Emperor's hologram faded away.

AFTER ARRIVING at the creature's house on Dagobah, Luke was impatient. 'Oh, I don't know what I'm doing here. We're wasting our time.'

The creature looked disappointed as he said, 'I cannot teach him. The boy has no patience.'

From nowhere, Ben's voice answered, 'He will learn patience.'

Luke suddenly realised the truth and gasped, 'Yoda!'

Yoda nodded.

'I *am* ready,' Luke said. 'I … Ben! I … I can be a Jedi. Ben, tell him I'm ready.'

Yoda finally agreed, and not long afterward, Luke's muscles strained as he stood on his hands, with Yoda perched on his right foot.

'Feel the Force flow through you,' Yoda intoned.

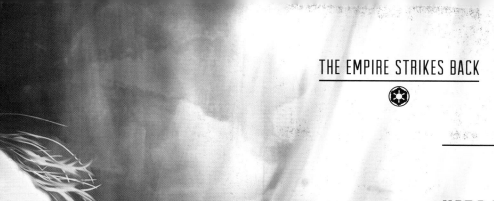

YODA WAS RIDING in a pack strapped to Luke's back.

'Beware of the dark side. Anger … fear … aggression. Easily they flow, quick to join you in a fight. If once you start down the dark path, forever will it dominate your destiny, consume you it will.'

'Vader,' Luke said, knowing what Yoda meant. 'Is the dark side stronger?'

Yoda answered, 'No … no … no. Easier, more seductive.'

'But how am I to know the good side from the bad?'

'You will know,' Yoda assured him. 'When you are calm, at peace. Passive. A Jedi uses the Force for knowledge and defence, never for attack.'

LUKE SENSED SOMETHING

strange and turned to see a huge, dead, black tree.

'That place …' Yoda said from his seat, 'is strong with the dark side of the Force. In you must go.'

Luke started for the tree, holding his blaster in his hand. His lightsaber hung off his belt.

'Your weapons …' Yoda said. 'You will not need them.'

Luke ignored the Jedi Master. He brushed aside some hanging vines, then lowered himself into a hole. In the darkness, he could barely make out anything. Then he saw something.

Darth Vader.

Luke swung his lightsaber – and cut off Vader's head.

Luke stared at the helmet as the smoke cleared to reveal a face: the face was Luke's own.

Yoda knew that it had been a test. And that Luke had failed.

STANDING INSIDE the asteroid cave, Han, Leia and Chewbacca tried to find the creatures that were attaching themselves to the *Falcon*. Chewbacca pointed at a leathery winged creature attached to the *Falcon*'s cockpit – a mynock.

When they fired their blasters in the cave, the mynocks flew away – but the cave itself shook violently. 'Wait a minute …' Han said. He fired again.

The whole cave rumbled and tilted hard to the side.

Han shouted, 'Let's get out of here!'

They ran back to the *Falcon*. Han flew the ship towards a row of jagged white teeth that surrounded the cave's entrance.

'This is no cave,' Han said.

Chewbacca howled as the *Falcon* passed – just barely – between two of the gigantic white teeth. The monster space slug tried for another bite but missed. The *Falcon* was too fast.

ON THE BRIDGE of his giant starship, Darth Vader approached six bizarre figures. They were bounty hunters. The menacing lizard's name was Bossk. There was Dengar, a brutal-looking man in battered armour; IG-88, an assassin droid; Zuckuss, an insect-like alien; and his partner, 4-LOM, a late-model protocol droid.

Finally, there was the bounty hunter who was widely regarded as the most dangerous of all: Boba Fett.

Darth Vader said, 'There will be a substantial reward for the one who finds the *Millennium Falcon*. But I want them alive.' Vader extended a black-gloved finger at Boba Fett and said, 'No disintegrations.'

WHILE PRACTICING, Luke noticed that his X-wing starfighter was slowly sinking into the swamp. 'Oh, no,' he said. 'We'll never get it out now.'

'So certain are you,' Yoda replied. 'Always with you it cannot be done. Hear you nothing that I say?'

Luke thought his ship was much too heavy to lift with the Force.

'Size matters not,' Yoda said. 'Judge me by my size, do you? Mm?'

Yoda then raised his small hand and the starfighter rose out of the water and landed on the shore. Luke knelt before the Jedi Master and gasped, 'I don't believe it!'

With a touch of sadness in his voice, Yoda said, 'That is why you fail.'

AS THE *FALCON* sped away from the Empire's ships, another ship was secretly following it: *Slave I*, which belonged to the bounty hunter Boba Fett.

Not long afterward, the *Falcon* was nearing Cloud City, where the crew hoped they'd be safe from the Empire. Two cloud cars suddenly swooped into view. Han said into the comlink, 'I'm trying to reach Lando Calrissian.'

The nearest cloud car fired a blaster cannon. 'Whoa!' Han shouted. 'Wait a minute!'

'You will not deviate from your present course,' the cloud car pilot commanded sternly.

Leia said to Han, 'I thought you knew this person.'

Chewie barked and growled at Han, who replied, 'Well, that was a long time ago. I'm sure he's forgotten about that.'

THE *FALCON* TOUCHED DOWN

at Cloud City. At the end of the platform, a door slid up to reveal two men and some guards. One of the men was Lando Calrissian, who said to Han, 'How are you doing, you old pirate? What are you doing here?'

'Ahh ... repairs,' Han said, indicating the *Falcon*.

Han and Lando laughed as the group walked through the city. C-3PO heard a familiar beeping sound coming from an open doorway. Curious, he entered.

'Who are you?' snapped a cold voice.

C-3PO said, 'Oh, I'm terribly sorry. I ... I didn't mean to intrude.' Then he threw his arms up and cried, 'No!'

There was a sudden explosion of blaster fire and C-3PO was blown to pieces.

135

LUKE HAD A VISION of Han and Leia in pain. He had to go to them. He was about to board his X-wing when Yoda stopped him. 'You must complete the training,' Yoda told him.

'I can't keep the vision out of my head,' Luke replied. He was afraid for his friends.

'Patience,' a shimmering Ben Kenobi said. 'If you choose to face Vader, you will do it alone. I cannot interfere.'

'I understand,' Luke said.

'Strong is Vader,' Yoda added. 'Mind what you have learned. Save you it can.'

'I will,' Luke said as he pulled on his helmet. 'And I'll return. I promise.'

The X-wing ascended into the night sky.

Yoda sighed and shook his head sadly. 'Reckless is he,' he said. 'Now matters are worse.'

Ben replied, 'That boy is our last hope.'

But then Yoda said mysteriously, 'No. There is another.'

CHEWBACCA SEARCHED everywhere and finally found C-3PO in several pieces. He was showing Han and Leia what he had found when Lando arrived to invite them to eat with him.

As they walked down a hallway, Han asked, 'Aren't you afraid the Empire's going to find out about this little operation and shut you down?'

Lando stopped at a pair of closed double doors and said, 'I've just made a deal that will keep the Empire out of here forever.'

The doors opened to reveal Darth Vader!

Han fired at Vader, who raised his black-gloved hand and deflected the bolt. A figure stepped out from an alcove behind Vader. It was Boba Fett. The rebels were prisoners.

LUKE'S X-WING STARFIGHTER raced across space. 'Just hang on,' Luke said to R2-D2. 'We're almost there.'

Meanwhile, Chewbacca was locked in a Cloud City prison cell where a high-pitched siren was screeching. He roared in protest. Finally, the siren stopped. The Wookiee shook his head and moaned. Exhausted, he went to a case that contained C-3PO's disconnected parts. Chewbacca picked up the droid's head. He stuck C-3PO's head into the torso's neck socket and began to reconnect the wires and adjust the circuits.

The lights in C-3PO's eyes sparked on and then flickered out. Chewbacca squeezed a circuit as he pulled a wire, and the droid's eyes lit up again. Maybe Chewie could repair his friend!

SOLO'S CRIES OF PAIN filtered through the closed door. A moment later, the door slid open and Darth Vader exited. Brushing past Lando, Vader faced Boba Fett and said, 'You may take Captain Solo to Jabba the Hutt after I have Skywalker.'

'He's no good to me dead,' Boba Fett said, following Vader into a corridor with Lando.

'He will not be permanently damaged,' Vader assured him.

'What about Leia and the Wookiee?' Lando asked.

'They must never again leave this city,' Vader told him.

Lando was stunned. 'That was never a condition of our agreement, nor was giving Han to this bounty hunter!'

'Perhaps you think you're being treated unfairly,' Vader said as he got into a lift tube.

Lando rubbed his throat as if someone were trying to choke him. 'No,' he said.

'Good,' Vader said.

The lift tube door slid shut.

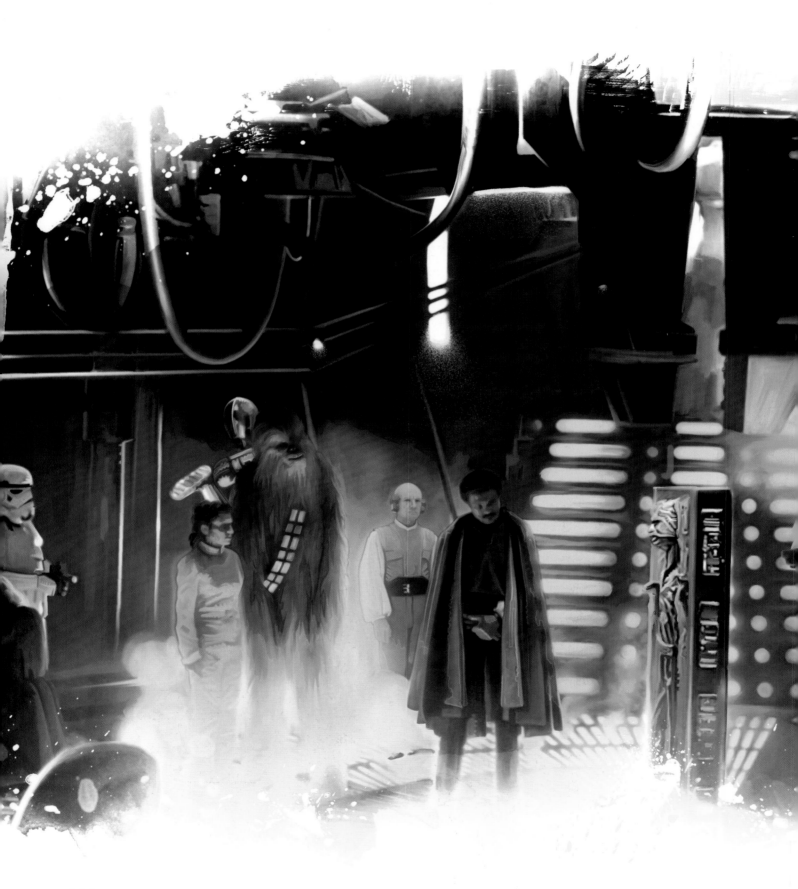

STEAM BLASTED AND BILLOWED

from various vents in the carbon-freeze chamber. Boba Fett led the procession, followed by Han Solo, whose hands were manacled, then Princess Leia and Chewbacca. Strapped to the Wookiee's back, a cargo net carried C-3PO, who was still in parts but able to see and talk.

Han came to a stop behind Lando and said, 'What's going on … buddy?'

Without turning to face Han, Lando said, 'You're being put into carbon freeze.'

Chewbacca and Princess Leia were very upset. The stormtroopers pulled Han away and put him on the carbon-freeze platform.

Leia called out, 'I love you!'

Han said, 'I know.'

An Ugnaught threw a switch, and Han was lowered into the steaming pit.

CHEWBACCA WHIMPERED as large tongs locked on to the solid block of carbonite, then raised it to the platform. Han Solo was frozen solid within it. Lando knelt beside the carbonite block and checked the life systems. Vader said, 'Well, Calrissian, did he survive?'

'Yes, he's alive,' Lando replied. 'And in perfect hibernation.'

Vader turned to Boba Fett and said, 'He's all yours, bounty hunter.'

An Imperial officer arrived and said, 'Skywalker has just landed, my lord.'

'Good,' Vader said. 'See to it that he finds his way in here. Calrissian, take the princess and the Wookiee to my ship.'

Lando was outraged. 'You said they'd be left in the city under my supervision!'

'I am altering the deal,' Vader said. 'Pray I don't alter it any further.'

LUKE LANDED HIS X-WING and sneaked into Cloud City. R2-D2 tried to follow him, but a moment after Luke entered a room, a door slid down, leaving the little droid alone. Meanwhile, Leia and Chewbacca were being led through another corridor by stormtroopers when a group of Cloud City guards rescued them.

Surprised, Leia asked Lando, 'What do you think you're doing?'

The moment Chewbacca's binders were unlocked, he wrapped his massive hands around Lando's neck.

'I had no choice …' Lando gasped.

Chewbacca tightened his grip, forcing Lando to his knees. Lando gasped and whispered, 'I'm just trying to help … There's still a chance to save Han …'

TWO GUARDS GUIDED the floating carbonite block up *Slave I*'s landing ramp and into the ship. 'Put Captain Solo in the cargo hold,' Boba Fett said.

Not far behind, Leia, Lando and Chewbacca were racing down a corridor towards the *Slave I* when C-3PO spotted a familiar droid. 'Artoo!' he cried. 'Hurry! We're trying to save Han from the bounty hunter!'

R2-D2 whistled frantically.

'Well, at least you're still in one piece!' C-3PO replied, bouncing along on the Wookiee's back. 'Look what happened to me!'

When they reached the landing platform, *Slave I* was already lifting off. Chewbacca fired his blaster rifle, but it was too late.

'This way,' Lando cried, and led them in another direction, towards the *Millennium Falcon*.

Stormtroopers followed and tried to blast them, but the rebels fought back and made it to their ship. The *Falcon* lifted off and roared away.

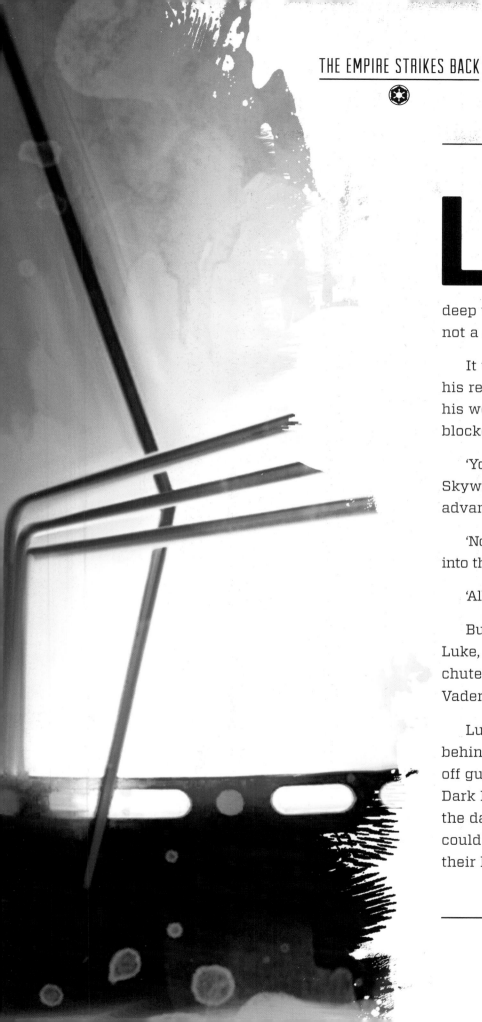

LUKE STEPPED OFF the turbolift into the carbon-freeze chamber.

'The Force is with you,' a deep voice rumbled. 'But you are not a Jedi yet.'

It was Darth Vader. He ignited his red lightsaber. Luke raised his weapon and swung, but Vader blocked the blow with ease.

'Your destiny lies with me, Skywalker,' Vader said as he advanced.

'No!' Luke cried, then backed right into the open carbon-freeze chute.

'All too easy,' Vader said to himself.

But then Vader looked up to see Luke, who had leaped out of the chute just in time. 'Impressive ...' Vader commented.

Luke leaped again and landed behind Vader, who was caught off guard as Luke lashed out. The Dark Lord snarled as he fell into the darkness below. Although Luke could no longer see Vader, he knew their battle was not yet over.

INSIDE A REACTOR SHAFT,

Luke moved carefully. But Vader leaped out from the shadows with his lightsaber blazing. He was relentless and drove Luke to the end of the platform above a seemingly bottomless pit.

Luke swung wildly and Vader cut off his hand.

'You are beaten,' Vader said. 'Join me and I will complete your training.'

Luke screamed, 'I'll never join you!'

'If only you knew the power of the dark side,' Vader said. 'Obi-Wan never told you what happened to your father.'

'He told me enough!' Luke said. 'He told me you killed him.'

'No,' Vader said. 'I am your father.'

Luke's eyes widened. 'No,' he cried. 'That's not true! That's impossible!'

'Luke. Join me, and together we can rule the galaxy as father and son.'

Then Vader watched in astonishment as Luke let himself fall into the endless reactor shaft.

LUKE SAILED into an exhaust pipe, where a trapdoor opened beneath him, dropping him through a hole onto an electronic weather vane on the underside of Cloud City. Below Luke was nothing but clouds.

'Leia!' he cried out with the Force. 'Hear me! Leia!'

Inside the *Falcon*, Leia heard Luke's voice. The *Falcon* looped around and sped back. The moment the *Falcon*'s hatch was beneath him, Luke dropped into Lando's arms.

On the bridge of his Star Destroyer, Vader watched the *Falcon* attempt to evade the TIE fighters. He said aloud, 'Luke.'

On the *Falcon*, Luke responded, 'Father.'

The hyperdrive kicked in and the *Falcon* blasted into hyperspace.

Vader was left looking into the darkness of empty space.

THE REBEL FLEET was gathered in space. Luke and Leia were on board a medical ship. They were standing with R2-D2 and the fully repaired C-3PO. From Luke's comlink, Lando's voice said, 'Princess, we'll find Han. I promise.'

Luke had a new mechanical hand. He put his arm around Leia's shoulders. R2-D2 whistled as the *Falcon* flew out of sight, with Lando and Chewbacca on board.

The future had once seemed so promising to Luke, but now everything was uncertain and complicated. Luke Skywalker had much to think about, but the rebels would continue their fight against the evil Empire...

STAR WARS

EPISODE VI
RETURN OF THE JEDI

LUKE SKYWALKER HAS RETURNED to his home planet of Tatooine in an attempt to rescue his friend Han Solo from the clutches of the vile gangster Jabba the Hutt.

Little does Luke know that the Galactic Empire has secretly begun construction on a new armoured space station even more powerful than the first dreaded Death Star.

When completed, this ultimate weapon will spell certain doom for the small band of rebels struggling to restore freedom to the galaxy ...

THE SECOND Death Star was far from finished. An Imperial Star Destroyer arrived near the building site; then a shuttle and two TIE fighters dropped out of the Star Destroyer's main hangar. As the shuttle and its escorts travelled towards the Death Star, its captain spoke into a comlink: 'Command station, we're starting our approach. Deactivate the security shield.'

On the shuttle, Darth Vader peered through a window at the monstrous space station. He was thinking about his son, Luke Skywalker ... and how he could convert him to the dark side.

THE DEATH STAR'S commanding officer, Moff Jerjerrod, greeted Darth Vader.

'Lord Vader,' Jerjerrod said. 'This is an unexpected pleasure. We're honoured by your presence.'

'You may dispense with the pleasantries, Commander,' Vader said, not breaking his stride as he moved past the gathered troops. 'I'm here to put you back on schedule.'

'I tell you, this station will be operational as planned.'

Turning to face Jerjerrod, Vader said, 'The Emperor is most displeased with your apparent lack of progress.'

Jerjerrod looked nervous. 'We shall double our efforts,' he said.

'I hope so, Commander, for your sake. The Emperor is not as forgiving as I am.'

Vader turned and walked out of the hangar, leaving Jerjerrod to prepare for the Emperor's arrival.

ON TATOOINE, C-3PO and R2-D2 were making their way up a hill to Jabba the Hutt's palace. They were part of a plan to rescue Han Solo, who had been frozen in carbonite and delivered to Jabba by a bounty hunter named Boba Fett.

'Of course I'm worried,' the protocol droid said. 'Lando Calrissian and poor Chewbacca never returned from this awful place.'

C-3PO hesitantly approached the gigantic door and knocked. Suddenly, there was a metallic grinding noise and the door began to rise. The door was still opening as R2-D2 scooted under it and into the citadel's dark, cavernous entry.

'Artoo, wait,' C-3PO called. 'Oh, dear!'

JABBA'S THRONE ROOM was
a dimly lit chamber that was
crawling with grotesque creatures.
Jabba himself rested his bulky
form on a broad dais.

C-3PO bowed and said, 'Good
morning.'

R2-D2 rotated his dome and
projected his holographic message
of Luke Skywalker, who said:
'Greetings, Exalted One. I am Luke
Skywalker, Jedi Knight and friend
to Captain Solo. I seek an audience
with Your Greatness to bargain for
Solo's life.'

Hearing this, Jabba laughed
heartily.

Luke's hologram continued. 'As
a token of my goodwill, I present
to you a gift: these two droids.'

Hearing this, C-3PO muttered,
'We're doomed.'

JABBA WAS HAVING A PARTY.

Female aliens danced to the rhythms of the Max Rebo Band. On the bandstand, Max Rebo – a blue-skinned Ortolan – performed the music. While the music played, a Twi'lek named Oola danced, too.

Jabba asked Oola to come sit with him. When she refused, Jabba slammed his fist down on a button. A trapdoor opened beneath her and Oola plummeted through the floor.

While Jabba's friends looked down through the grating to watch Oola meet her doom, C-3PO shook his head and turned away. He glanced at the carbonite form of Han Solo, which was hanging on the wall, and wondered if he'd ever leave Jabba's palace in one piece.

LATER, TWO MYSTERIOUS FIGURES entered the throne room: a bounty hunter named Boushh held a leash that led to the neck of the second figure, a tall, furry Wookiee.

On his dais, Jabba grinned and said, 'At last we have the mighty Chewbacca.'

Speaking through C-3PO to translate, Boushh said, 'I want fifty thousand. No less.'

Jabba flew into a rage. C-3PO spoke for Jabba: 'The mighty Jabba asks why he must pay fifty thousand.'

Boushh's left hand revealed a metal orb.

Cringing, C-3PO cried out, 'Because he's holding a thermal detonator!'

Jabba began to laugh. 'This bounty hunter is my kind of scum … fearless and inventive.'

A pair of Gamorrean guards grabbed Chewbacca and hauled him out of the room.

NIGHT FELL ON TATOOINE. Boushh stepped silently through the throne room. The bounty hunter looked up at where Han Solo hung on the wall, frozen in carbonite. Boushh pressed a button and then watched bright energy spill out of the carbon shell. The carbonite melted, and Han fell forward, collapsing on the sandy floor.

Boushh knelt beside him.

'I can't see,' Han said.

'Your eyesight will return in time,' Boushh replied.

Han shook. 'Who are you?'

Boushh removed his leather-and-metal helmet – it was Princess Leia! She said, 'Someone who loves you.'

'Leia!'

But then they both heard a low, rumbling laugh. A curtain slid back behind them to reveal Jabba the Hutt and his chortling minions. They were trapped!

ONCE AGAIN, there was silence in Jabba's throne room. Leia, eyes closed, sat beside Jabba's slumbering form. She had replaced Oola as Jabba's slave dancer.

Jabba's servant Bib Fortuna was also awake. Hearing the sound of footsteps descending the stairway from the main entrance, he saw Luke coming down. He told Luke to leave immediately.

Luke simply said, 'I must speak with Jabba.'

Hearing those words, Leia opened her eyes and sat up. *Luke!*

Luke stared hard at Bib and said, 'You will take me to Jabba now!'

Bib did not realise that Luke was using the Force to influence his thoughts.

He let Luke approach the dais. From behind Jabba, C-3PO cried out, 'At last! Master Luke's come to rescue me!'

JABBA'S HEAVY EYELIDS slid
back and he let out a wet snort.
'You weak-minded fool!' Jabba said,
scowling at Bib. 'He's using an old
Jedi mind trick.'

Luke spotted the disguised
Lando among Jabba's guards.
Staring hard at Jabba, he said, 'You
will bring Captain Solo and the
Wookiee to me.'

Jabba laughed. 'Your mind
powers will not work on me, boy.'

C-3PO saw that Luke was
standing on the trapdoor. 'Master
Luke,' the droid called out, 'you're – '

But Jabba interrupted: 'I shall
enjoy watching you die.'

A guard's blaster suddenly
jumped out of its holster and flew
into Luke's waiting hand. As Luke
raised the blaster, Jabba triggered
the trapdoor – and both Luke and
a Gamorrean guard plunged into
the pit!

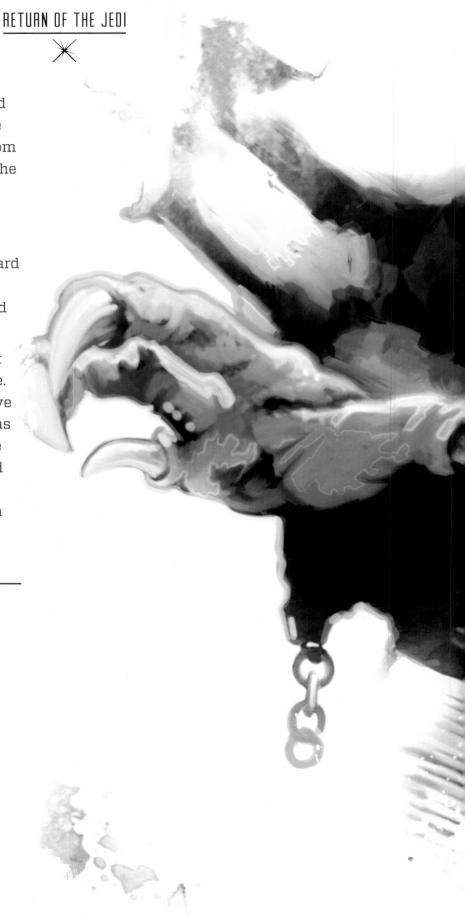

LUKE LANDED in a pile of skeletons. A horrific growl echoed from a cave beyond the door. The Gamorrean started squealing. From above, C-3PO cried out, 'Oh, no! The rancor!'

Lurching into the pit on two powerful legs, the rancor had an enormous fanged mouth. The guard tried to run away, but the rancor gobbled him up – and then turned for Luke.

The rancor swiped at him, but Luke dodged and ran for the cave. He picked up a skull from the cave floor and hurled it. The rancor was just ducking its head through the doorway when the skull smashed against the control panel. The heavy iron door crashed down on the rancor. The rancor was dead.

JABBA WAS ENRAGED and sentenced Luke and his friends to be fed to the Sarlacc, which lived in a pit in the desert. Not long afterward, a skiff flew over the desert. It was loaded with Jabba's guards – including Lando in disguise – and three bound captives: Luke, Han and Chewbacca. Leia was a prisoner in Jabba's sail barge, which flew next to the skiff.

When they arrived, at Jabba's command C-3PO picked up a comlink and announced, 'Victims of the almighty Sarlacc: should any of you wish to beg for mercy, the great Jabba the Hutt will now listen to your pleas.'

'Jabba!' Luke called out. 'This is your last chance. Free us or die.'

Jabba and his cronies were almost overcome by their own mocking laughter.

A GUARD PRODDED LUKE to the edge of the plank directly above the Sarlacc's gaping maw. Luke looked at R2-D2 on the barge's deck and gave him a signal. Luke then bounced off the plank skyward. R2-D2 simultaneously launched a lightsaber from his dome. Luke landed on the skiff and caught his lightsaber. He instantly ignited it and began to battle!

The Wookiee barked anxiously as Lando was knocked over the side of the skiff. Fett, who was on the barge, fired the jets on his backpack and blasted away.

As Chewbacca untied Han's bonds, Fett landed on the prisoners' skiff and brought up his blaster rifle. He was going to shoot Luke!

BEFORE FETT COULD FIRE,

Luke spun with his lightsaber and hacked off the blaster's barrel. Chewbacca barked at Han.

'Boba Fett! Where?' Han answered. He was holding a spear that Chewbacca had directed him to pick up from the floor of the skiff, but he still couldn't see.

He turned blindly, swinging the spear hard. By sheer luck, it hit the bounty hunter's backpack. Fett was launched from the skiff like a missile. His bounced off the side of the sail barge and tumbled into the Sarlacc's mouth. A moment later, the Sarlacc burped loudly.

Meanwhile, on the sail barge, Leia leaped up behind Jabba, draping her chain over his head and around his neck. She pulled and pulled. A few moments later Jabba was dead.

BECAUSE JABBA'S GUARDS

were still firing a huge cannon at Luke's friends, Luke leaped from the skiff to the side of the sail barge. The gunners were about to release another barrage when Luke leaped onto the barge's deck. He activated his lightsaber and made quick work of them, then moved towards the other guards, cutting down their weapons and deflecting laser bolts back at the shooters.

During all the commotion, R2-D2 had managed to avoid being trampled and had returned to Jabba's banquet room to find Leia still chained to Jabba. R2-D2 extended his laser torch and fired a controlled burst at the chain, neatly cutting it in two and freeing Leia.

'Come on,' Leia said. 'We gotta get out of here.'

C-3PO HURRIED AFTER R2-D2, heading for the deck. Leia was already there, and she saw Luke fighting several guards. He caught sight of Leia and said, 'Get the gun!'

Leia ran to the large laser cannon and climbed onto the weapon's turret platform. As she began to swivel the cannon around, Luke raised his lightsaber to fend off another attacker and yelled, 'Point it at the deck!'

Luke ran to her. He took hold of a rope, then kicked the trigger of the laser cannon. The cannon fired into the deck as Luke and Leia swung to the skiff, joining Han, Chewie and Lando.

ON THE SKIFF, Luke said, 'Let's go! And don't forget the droids.'

Lando guided the skiff until they saw C-3PO's legs sticking out of the sand. Two large electromagnets hoisted both droids up just before a great explosion tore through the barge. A chain of explosions followed as Jabba's sail barge collapsed in a fiery blaze.

Soon afterward, Luke was alone piloting his X-wing, and Han and the others were on board the *Falcon*. After leaving Tatooine behind, the two ships veered off in different directions.

'Meet you back at the fleet,' Luke said into his helmet's comlink.

Han responded, 'Hey, Luke, thanks for coming after me.'

Luke smiled, then angled his ship for a distant star – Dagobah.

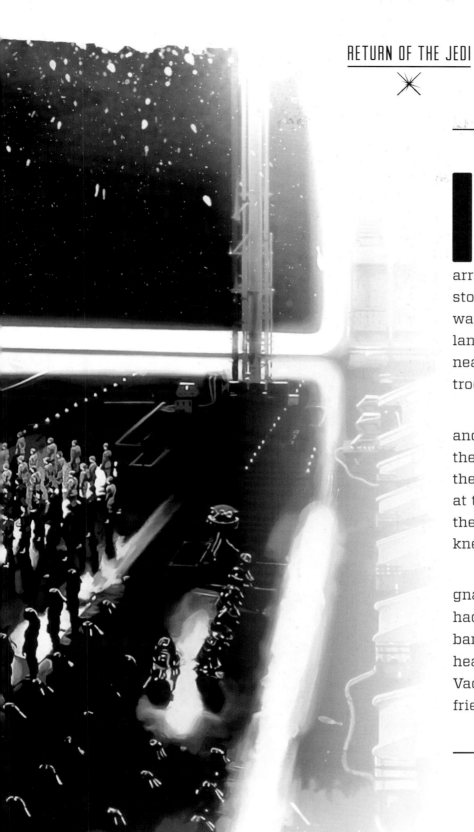

I **N A GREAT DISPLAY** of the Empire's might, thousands of TIE fighters travelled in orbit of the Death Star to mark the arrival of Emperor Palpatine. Vader stood in a large docking bay and watched the Emperor's shuttle as it landed. The docking bay was filled nearly to capacity with Imperial troops in tight formation.

The landing ramp descended and Vader watched six members of the Royal Guard disembark. After the Royal Guard took their positions at the base of the landing ramp, the Emperor emerged. Darth Vader kneeled.

Hunched and walking with a gnarled cane, Emperor Palpatine had ghastly, withered features barely visible under the hood of his heavy black cloak. Stopping before Vader, the Emperor said, 'Rise, my friend.'

VADER ROSE TO WALK alongside the Emperor, who moved slowly past the long rows of troops.

'The Death Star will be completed on schedule,' Vader reported.

'You have done well, Lord Vader,' the Emperor replied, his voice a decrepit rasp. 'And now I sense you wish to continue your search for young Skywalker.'

'Yes, my master.'

'Patience, my friend. In time, he will seek you out. And when he does, you must bring him before *me*. He has grown *strong*. Only together can we turn him to the dark side of the Force.'

Vader said, 'As you wish.'

The Emperor said, 'Everything is proceeding as I have foreseen.' He cackled to himself, and the evil sound echoed across the docking bay.

'YOU HAVE DONE WELL,
LORD VADER.'

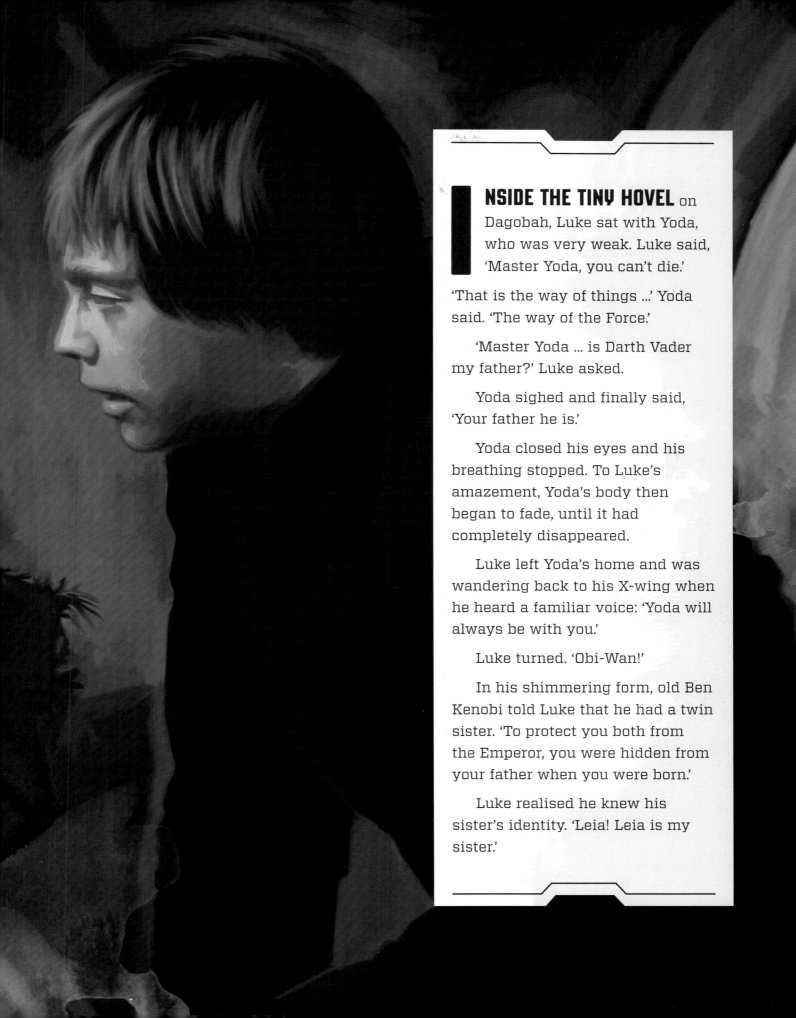

INSIDE THE TINY HOVEL on Dagobah, Luke sat with Yoda, who was very weak. Luke said, 'Master Yoda, you can't die.'

'That is the way of things …' Yoda said. 'The way of the Force.'

'Master Yoda … is Darth Vader my father?' Luke asked.

Yoda sighed and finally said, 'Your father he is.'

Yoda closed his eyes and his breathing stopped. To Luke's amazement, Yoda's body then began to fade, until it had completely disappeared.

Luke left Yoda's home and was wandering back to his X-wing when he heard a familiar voice: 'Yoda will always be with you.'

Luke turned. 'Obi-Wan!'

In his shimmering form, old Ben Kenobi told Luke that he had a twin sister. 'To protect you both from the Emperor, you were hidden from your father when you were born.'

Luke realised he knew his sister's identity. 'Leia! Leia is my sister.'

ABOARD THE REBEL ALLIANCE flagship, Luke was reunited with all his friends. Mon Mothma, leader of the Rebellion, spoke to the assembled rebels: 'The time for our attack has come.'

Holograms of the Death Star and a green orb appeared.

'We also know that the weapon systems of this Death Star are not yet operational,' Mon Mothma added.

But the Death Star was protected by a shield projected from the nearby forest moon. 'A strike team will land on the moon and deactivate the shield generator,' said General Madine.

Then the rebel fleet would blow up the Death Star.

Han, Chewie, Luke and Leia volunteered to deactivate the shield generator on the forest moon. Lando would pilot the *Falcon* against the Death Star.

R2-D2 beeped a singsong observation.

C-3PO shuddered and replied, '"Exciting" is hardly the word I would choose.'

193

HAN SAT BEHIND the controls of the stolen Imperial shuttle as his friends looked on nervously. Their shuttle dropped out of hyperspace – right into the Imperial fleet.

From the shuttle's comlink came the voice of an Imperial controller: 'We have you on our screen now. Please identify.'

Han said, 'Shuttle *Tydirium* requesting deactivation of the deflector shield.'

Luke was suddenly filled with dread. He sensed Vader. 'I'm endangering the mission,' Luke said. 'I shouldn't have come.'

'Don't get jittery,' Han said to Luke. But he was nervous, too.

Then the controller spoke again: 'Shuttle *Tydirium*, deactivation of the shield will commence immediately. Follow your present course.'

'Okay!' Han said, glancing back at his friends. 'I told you it was gonna work. No problem.'

He flew the shuttle past the Death Star, down to the forest moon of Endor.

AFTER LANDING on the forest moon, the rebels approached a clearing. Luke saw two scout troopers on speeder bikes zooming away. If they reported the rebels, the whole mission would be a failure. So Luke and Leia jumped on another speeder bike and took off after them.

Catching up to one of them, Luke leaped to the other speeder and threw off the trooper. But the second trooper fired and hit Leia's bike. Luckily, she dove off before her bike slammed into a tree.

Another trooper attacked Luke, pushing his bike towards a huge tree. Luke dived off, but he got back up quickly and ignited his lightsaber. When the scout zoomed towards him, Luke cut off the front of his bike, which then slammed into a tree in a fiery explosion.

AN EWOK, a furry native of the forest, found Leia lying on the ground. His name was Wicket. He poked her with his spear. Princess Leia woke up and said, 'Cut it out!'

Wicket jumped back.

'I'm not gonna hurt you,' Leia said gently. 'You want something to eat?'

She removed a bit of food from her pocket and held it out to him. After sniffing it carefully, Wicket took it from Leia's hand and ate it.

'Come on,' Leia said. 'Let's get out of here.'

As they moved into the forest, Wicket tugged at Leia's arm. Figuring that her newfound friend knew his way around better than she did, Leia decided to follow him.

ON THE DEATH STAR, two stood watch in the Emperor's throne room. The turbolift door slid open and Darth Vader entered. The Emperor said, 'I told you to remain on the command ship.'

'A small rebel force has penetrated the shield and landed on Endor,' Vader replied. 'My son is with them. I have *felt* him, my master.'

'Strange that I have not,' the Emperor said warily. Leaning forward in his chair, he continued. 'I wonder if your feelings on this matter are clear, Lord Vader.'

'They are clear, my master.'

'Then you must go to the Sanctuary Moon and wait for him.'

Vader was sceptical. 'He will come to me?'

'I have foreseen it,' the Emperor said.

CHEWBACCA SNIFFED at the air and growled.

'What is it, Chewie?' Han asked.

Chewbacca barked. Luke, Han, Chewie and the droids were looking for Princess Leia. The Wookiee led them to a dead animal carcass. Unable to resist, Chewbacca reached for the carcass – which triggered a trap! The next thing they knew, they were lifted high above the ground in a net. R2-D2 quickly extended a circular saw and cut through the net. They all fell to the ground. As they got up, they were surrounded by many Ewoks armed with stone-tipped spears and knives.

At the sight of C-3PO, however, they began to chant and bow down before the golden droid. They seemed to think Threepio was some kind of god. Unfortunately, the Ewoks didn't think much of C-3PO's friends.

● ● ● ● ● ● ● ●

A PROCESSION WALKED THROUGH the dark forest with their prisoners, each of whom was tied to a long pole carried on the shoulders of Ewoks. Soon they reached a village. Leia and Wicket emerged from a large hut. Leia told the Ewoks that the prisoners were her friends and they should be set free. But the Ewoks refused.

Luke said, 'Threepio, tell them if they don't do as you wish, you'll become angry and use your magic.'

Then Luke used the Force to levitate C-3PO's throne. The Ewoks fell back in terror and released their prisoners. Later, the Ewok tribe listened in amazement to C-3PO's story of the rebels' adventures against the Empire.

The Ewok elders talked with C-3PO, who then exclaimed, 'Wonderful! We are now a part of the tribe.'

LEIA FOLLOWED LUKE OUTSIDE. She asked, 'Luke, what's wrong?'

Luke hesitated, then said, 'Vader is here … now, on this moon. That's why I have to go. I have to face him.'

'Why?'

'He's my father.'

'Your father?' Leia gasped.

'There's more,' Luke said. 'It won't be easy for you to hear it, but you must. If I don't make it back, you're the only hope for the Alliance. The Force is strong in my family. My father has it … I have it …' Then he looked at Leia as he added, 'And my sister has it.'

Leia stared into Luke's eyes. 'Yes,' Luke said. 'It's you, Leia.'

'I know. Somehow … I've always known,' she said.

Luke hugged his sister, then walked off into the forest.

THE REBEL ALLIANCE FLEET prepared for their flight to the Death Star. Lando Calrissian sat in the cockpit of the *Millennium Falcon* with his copilot, a Sullustan named Nien Nunb. Behind them, two rebel soldiers checked the *Falcon*'s navigational and shield controls.

Lando guided the *Falcon* past the larger battle cruisers. He was followed by a group of starfighters that included X-wings, A-wings, B-wings and Y-wings.

'Admiral, we're in position,' Lando reported into his comlink. The Mon Calamari Admiral Ackbar was in charge of the Death Star assault.

Admiral Ackbar's voice came from the comm: 'All groups assume attack coordinates.'

Nien Nunb was nervous, but Lando said, 'My friend's down there. He'll have that shield down on time.'

Then the entire rebel armada made the jump to hyperspace.

THE FLEET DROPPED OUT of hyperspace and the rebel ships headed straight for the Death Star. From his command cruiser, Admiral Ackbar said, 'May the Force be with us.'

In the *Falcon*'s cockpit, Nien Nunb couldn't get a reading on the Death Star's energy shield. Lando said, 'We've got to be able to get *some* kind of a reading on that shield.'

Nien Nunb responded in his alien language, and Lando said, 'Well, how could they be jamming us if they don't know we're coming?' And then Lando realised the truth: the Empire *did* know they were coming. 'Break off the attack!' he yelled. 'The shield is still up.'

The *Falcon* and the rebel starfighters all veered off to avoid crashing into the energy shield.

Admiral Ackbar said, 'It's a trap!'

THE *FALCON* and the other ships had turned straight into an armada of Star Destroyers. Then Lando saw hundreds of TIE fighters, which were targeting the rebel fleet.

'There's too many of them!' a rebel pilot shouted. A moment later, his ship was struck by enemy fire and it exploded.

Flying through the battle, Lando ordered, 'Accelerate to attack speed!'

Suddenly, an explosion rocked the rebel fleet as a cruiser was blown apart. Lando was stunned. 'That blast came from the Death Star!' he exclaimed. 'That thing's operational!'

Admiral Ackbar said, 'All craft prepare to retreat.'

'Han will have that shield down,' Lando promised. 'We've got to give him more time.'

'THIS IS A REBEL THAT
SURRENDERED TO US.
HE WAS ARMED ONLY WITH THIS.'

AS VADER'S SHUTTLE touched down on the forest moon, a walker lurched towards the landing platform. Vader disembarked and the walker's hatch slid up to reveal ... Luke Skywalker.

An officer said, 'This is a rebel that surrendered to us. He was armed only with this.'

The officer handed Luke's lightsaber over to Vader.

Vader ignited the brilliant green blade. 'Your skills are complete. Indeed, you are powerful, as the Emperor has foreseen.'

'Search your feelings, Father,' Luke said. 'I feel the conflict within you. Let go of your hate.'

'It is too late for me, Son,' Vader replied. 'The Emperor will show you the true nature of the Force. He is your master now.'

'Then my father is truly dead,' Luke said sadly.

PRINCESS LEIA, HAN SOLO, CHEWBACCA and the rebel commandos broke into the bunker containing the controls for the shield generator. They were about to blow up the bunker when they were captured by Imperials! Their Imperial captors led them outside, where they were surrounded by over a hundred Imperial troops.

C-3PO called to the stormtroopers from the nearby forest, trying to get their attention. When a group of stormtroopers approached to take C-3PO prisoner, a band of Ewoks jumped down from the surrounding trees! The Ewoks carried clubs, stones, knives and spears. Their attack was swift and ferocious, and most of the stormtroopers fell without knowing what had hit them.

Han and Chewbacca used the distraction to run back into the bunker and place several explosive charges. Then Han ran out of the bunker shouting, 'Move! Move!'

Chewbacca and the other rebels ran for cover. A moment later, the bunker and the shield generator blew up in a series of explosions.

N THE HIGHEST TOWER of the Death Star, Darth Vader and Luke arrived in the Emperor's throne room. Vader handed Luke's lightsaber to his master.

'Welcome, young Skywalker,' the Emperor said. 'I'm looking forward to completing your training. In time you will call *me* Master.'

Luke moved fast, using the Force to call his lightsaber from where it sat on the Emperor's throne. He then engaged his father in a vicious duel. Luke drove Vader back to the stairway, beating him down.

'Good! Your hate has made you powerful,' the Emperor said, cackling. 'Now, fulfil your destiny and take your father's place at *my* side!'

Then Luke made a fateful decision. He flung aside his lightsaber and said, 'I'll never turn to the dark side. You've failed, Your Highness. I am a Jedi, like my father before me.'

THE EMPEROR SAID, 'If you will not be turned, you will be *destroyed*.' He raised his arms and extended his gnarled fingers towards Luke. Bolts of blue lightning shot from the Emperor's hands, and Luke was enveloped by crackling bands of energy. As the lightning burned his son, Vader struggled to his feet.

'Young *fool* ...,' the Emperor sneered, 'only now, at the end, do you understand.'

More blue lightning swept through Luke.

'Your feeble skills are no match for the *power* of the dark side,' the Emperor said.

Using the last of his strength, Luke lifted his arm and reached out towards Vader. 'Father, please,' Luke groaned. 'Help me.'

Preparing for a final deadly blast, the Emperor snarled, 'Now, young Skywalker ... you will die.'

LUKE WAS HIT by a wave of painful lightning. His screams echoed across the throne room.

Darth Vader continued to stand and watch. Then something changed. Despite all the terrible, unspeakable things he'd done in his life, he suddenly realised he could not allow the Emperor to kill his son. In that moment, he was no longer Darth Vader.

He was Anakin Skywalker.

He grabbed the Emperor from behind and hurled him into the shaft. The Emperor screamed as his he plunged into the pit. Then his body exploded, releasing dark energy and creating a rush of air up through the throne room.

Luke crawled the short distance to his father's side and pulled him away from the edge of the abyss.

ADMIRAL ACKBAR announced, 'The shield is down! Commence attack on the Death Star's main reactor.'

From the *Falcon*, Lando said, 'We're on our way!'

The *Falcon* zipped into the exhaust port with the other rebel fighters right behind. But three TIE fighters zoomed in after them – and they were quickly followed by a trio of dagger-winged TIE interceptors.

Lando adjusted a switch on his console, then said into his comlink, 'Now lock on to the strongest power source. It should be the power generator.'

As they continued to race for the reactor core, laser fire tore past them from behind. The X-wing at the rear of the group was hit, and it exploded in the tunnel.

I N A DEATH STAR HANGAR, Luke struggled to haul Darth Vader to the shuttle. Vader lay back against the ramp. From the corridor outside the hangar came the sound of more explosions.

'Luke,' Vader gasped, 'help me take this mask off.'

Slowly, Luke lifted the helmet off, and he saw his father's face for the first time.

Anakin smiled weakly and said, 'Now ... go, my son. Leave me.'

'No,' Luke said. 'You're coming with me. I've got to save you.'

Anakin smiled again. 'You already have, Luke. You were right.' Choking, he gasped, 'You were right about me. Tell your sister ... you were right.'

Anakin Skywalker was dead. Luke piloted the shuttle away from the Death Star.

THE *FALCON* **FLEW** into the Death Star's reactor core. Lando fired the missiles, which scored direct hits. Behind him, a TIE interceptor was vaporised. Just as the *Falcon* sped back into the tunnel, the entire reactor core was filled with super-heated gases that rushed after the starships.

Behind the *Falcon*, the wave of intense heat caught up with another TIE interceptor and the ship was transformed into a fireball. A mass of jet flame blasted out from the exhaust port just as the *Falcon* broke away from the Death Star.

Lando let out a loud victory cry and the Death Star exploded. The blast was so brilliant and enormous that it could be seen from the forest moon!

DARKNESS HAD FALLEN on the forest moon when Luke carried a flaming torch to the logs he'd stacked in a clearing. He set the torch to the logs and they began to burn. On top of the pyre lay his father's body.

Standing alone, Luke watched the fire and felt the heat of its blaze. The flames rose high into the night. Fireworks exploded overhead, and then starfighters streaked across the sky. Luke realised his allies were celebrating.

News of the Rebel Alliance victory had spread quickly across the galaxy, to Cloud City, Tatooine, Naboo and Coruscant.

When the pyre had burned out, Luke went to find his friends.

HIGH ABOVE the forest floor, a wild celebration was taking place in the Ewok village. All the rebels – even the droids – were dancing. Lando arrived and was greeted by Han and Chewbacca. Then Luke appeared, and his friends rushed to greet and embrace him.

Stepping away from the others, Luke gazed into the night and saw three shimmering apparitions: Yoda, Ben Kenobi and a younger Anakin Skywalker. Luke was right: he was a Jedi like his father before him. The apparitions smiled at Luke, silently telling him that the Force would be with him ... always.

Leia came to Luke's side and took his hand, then led him back to the others.

The celebration went on long into the night.

MAY THE FORCE BE WITH YOU!